This Butterfly Besitos book belongs to

....

BUTTERFLY BESITOS BOOKS
PRESENT BIBLICAL CONCEPTS
TO YOUNG CHILDREN
THROUGH ALLEGORY.

The Fruit Family

First published in the UK in 2019, by Pura Track Publishing.

Text Copyright © Torema Thompson, 2019.

Illustration Copyright © Nicole Dennis, 2019.

ISBN (Paperback): 978-1-9999616-2-6

The author believes that Galatians 5:22-23 reveals 'love' to be <u>the</u> fruit of the Spirit and that the 8 terms listed thereafter are expressions of love. However, as the purpose of this book is to help children to memorise and receive this passage of scripture in their heart, all 9 terms are depicted as "fruits" in this book.

The Fruit Family

Written by

Torema Thompson

Illustrated by

Nicole Dennis

But the fruit of the Spirit is <u>love</u>, <u>joy</u>, <u>peace</u>, <u>patience</u>, <u>kindness</u>, <u>goodness</u>, <u>faithfulness</u>, <u>gentleness</u>, and <u>temperance</u>.
There is no law against these things!

(Galatians 5:22-23)

A MIX BETWEEN THE NEW LIVING TRANSLATION AND KING JAMES VERSION

Meet the Fruit family.

Mr Fruit was the head of the family and he loved his wife, Mrs Fruit, very much.

Mrs Fruit was the mother of the family,
and she loved Mr Fruit very much.

Together they had nine children,
and they loved all their children very much!

Their eldest child was named Love.

Love was very obedient to her parents, and when her siblings came along, she taught them how to obey Mr and Mrs Fruit too.

(John 14:15)

Next came Joy.

She was always happy and unusually strong.

Joy helped her family whenever there was anything heavy that needed lifting...

...and she was always first to rise in the morning (usually with a song and a dance)!

(NEHEMIAH 8:10, PSALM 30:5, PSALM 30:11)

Shortly after Joy arrived,
the Fruit family lost their home in a fire.

It was a sad and hard time; however, it was also special because that was when Mrs Fruit became pregnant again...

...but this time with twins!

Their names were Peace and Patience, and Mr Fruit always
says, "the twins were birthed through the fire!"

(James 1:3-4, Philippians 4:6-7)

Shortly after the twins were born,
the Fruit family purchased a new house.

In their new house, Mr and Mrs Fruit had another girl!

Her name was Kindness.

Kindness was just what the Fruit family needed.

She was the helpful one, and the one who liked to buy gifts for the family, just because she could.

(GALATIANS 6:10)

When Mr and Mrs Fruit thought they were finished having children, along came Goodness.

The family loved Goodness,
and Goodness loved the family!

In fact, his favourite thing to do was to follow his family around wherever they went!

(PSALM 23:6)

After Goodness, along came Faithfulness.

If he said he would do something for you,
he always did just that!
He never broke a promise,
and he always kept his word.

(NUMBERS 23:19, HEBREWS 10:23)

Their last daughter was named Gentleness.

She knew just how to build everybody up.

When she was born,
the Fruit family became great in their town.

Everybody knew them, everybody loved them,
and Mr Fruit even became the mayor!

(PSALM 18:35)

Last, but not least, was their ninth child, Temperance.

He never lost his temper,
never ate too much,
never talked too much,
and seemed to always know what to do
at just the right time.

(James 1:19-20)

With nine children in total,
Mr and Mrs Fruit's family was complete.

Today, they still live in Kingdom Land,
enjoying a very FRUITFUL life indeed.

THE END

Questions to ask your children

1. Name the 9 children in the Fruit family.

2. Do you know what the Fruit children represent? (Read Galatians 5:22-23)

3. Which of the Fruit children do you feel is most like you?

4. Which fruit do you think Jesus still wants you to develop?

5. Choose one of the 9 Fruit children to discuss. Read the scripture at the bottom of the corresponding page and discuss what their characteristics mean to you.